VALENTINE VILLAINS

After waiting a bit longer, the princess knocked on the door. "Darling?" she called.

There was no response. She tried the door-knob, but it wouldn't turn. With a troubled look, the princess reached into her velvet bag and pulled out her little silver passkey. Then she opened the door—and gasped. The little room was empty!

The princess ran to the wide-open windows. Then, in a quiet rustle of taffeta, she sank to the floor in a faint.

VALENTINE VILLAINS

by Sarah Willson
illustrated by Artful Doodlers

Simon Spotlight
New York London Toronto Sydney

Based on the TV series *Totally Spies!* created by Marathon Animation as seen on Cartoon Network®. Series created by Vincent Chalvon-Demersay and David Michel

SIMON SPOTLIGHT
An imprint of Simon & Schuster Children's Publishing Division
1230 Avenue of the Americas, New York, New York 10020
Manufactured in the United States of America
First Edition 10 9 8 7 6 5 4 3 2 1
ISBN-13: 978-1-4169-0283-6
ISBN-10: 1-4169-0283-X
Library of Congress Catalog Card Number 2005002684

CHAPTER ONE

The Kingdom of Malrovia, 3:00 p.m.

"My darling," said the princess breathlessly. "Soon we shall be together always, and you shall be my prince. I will talk to my staff in just a few moments. The whole world will learn the news of our wedding plans tomorrow. How perfect that it is nearly Valentine's Day!" She clasped her hands together and sighed.

The tall, broad-shouldered young man

standing next to her twitched ever so slightly. But then he quickly smiled, showing perfectly even, white teeth. He looked into her love-struck eyes and murmured, "I shall always treasure everything that you have given me."

The princess sighed, her eyes shining.

He bent down and tenderly kissed her hand. Rising back up, he added casually, "Dearest, are you quite certain your personal secretary knows nothing of what is contained in the box of chocolates?"

"Oh, quite," she replied. Then she leaned closer to him and spoke in a low voice. "And anyway, the password is in code. Even if the chocolates fell into the wrong hands, the thief would have to know how to figure it out. My precious one, you and I are the only ones who know how." She smiled lovingly at him.

This time he smiled back broadly.

"Shall we go in and make the announcement together?" she asked.

"Wonderful idea, my love," he replied. "Give me a moment to tidy myself up a bit."

"Of course," she replied, though, as always, he looked perfect in his well-cut tuxedo. The princess watched adoringly as her true love stepped into the small powder room off the palace corridor.

But quite a few minutes went by, and he did not come back out. After waiting a bit longer, the princess knocked

on the door. "Darling?" she called.

There was no response. She tried the doorknob, but it wouldn't turn. With a troubled look, the princess reached into her velvet bag and pulled out her little silver passkey. Then she opened the door—and gasped. The little room was empty!

The princess ran to the wide-open windows. Then, in a quiet rustle of taffeta, she sank to the floor in a faint.

CHAPTER TWO

Beverly Hills Mall, 11:00 a.m.

"Okay, not to worry," said Sam. "We've gotten through plenty of crises before. There is absolutely no need to panic."

"Panic? Who's panicking?" replied Clover shrilly. "It's not as though the Valentine's Day dance is in two days, and like we have absolutely nothing to wear or anything. Oh, wait. Yes it is like that!"

"I think it's safe to say we are experiencing a fashion emergency," said Alex.

The girls were walking briskly through the Beverly Hills Mall on their way to their favorite store. It took a lot of willpower on

each of their parts not to break into a panicky run. With the Valentine's Dance at their school just days away, Clover had called Alex and Sam in the middle of a fashion meltdown, announcing she had nothing to wear. As it happened, Sam and Alex had been try-ing on everything in their own closets, scrambling to find something for the dance too.

"I thought I would wear my red halter dress, but then I realized my base tan has, like, totally faded!" said Clover.

"And I was going to show off my new blue dress until I saw Mandy buying the same one yesterday!" said Alex.

"Calm down, we're almost there," said Sam soothingly. "You know Fashion Victim will have just the right thing for all of us."

Fashion Victim was the girls' favorite store. They always managed to find the perfect thing to wear there. The girls quickly rounded a corner and screeched to a horrified halt. Fashion Victim was closed!

"Okay, so now it's time to panic," said Sam. "How can it be closed on a . . . WHOOOOOOPS!"

The large CLOSED sign hanging on the front

of the store had suddenly slid aside. Sam, Alex, and Clover were whisked through the opening. Then the floor gave way and they found themselves sliding down a long chute. They tumbled into a heap at the bottom, blinking in the bright lights.

Jerry stood in front of them.

CHAPTER THREE

WOOHP Headquarters, 11:07 a.m.

"Hello, ladies," Jerry said. He was their boss and head of the international secret agent organization known as WOOHP. WOOHP's mission was to battle the most dangerous villains the world had to offer. Although they were just teenagers, Sam, Clover, and Alex were three of Jerry's best spies.

"Okay, just once would it kill you to bring us here a little more stylishly?" said Clover, fixing her mussed hair. "Like, by limo?"

Jerry just gave her an amused smile and got straight down to business. He pressed a button on his desk; three chairs suddenly zoomed up from the floor, and the girls found themselves sitting down! A large screen descended noiselessly from the ceiling, and a young man's smiling face appeared.

The girls sighed and smiled back at the screen.

"Well, hello!" said Sam.

"Happy Valentine's Day to you!" Alex said, giggling.

"The hot-guy-o-meter dial is officially in the red zone!" said Clover.

"Girls. Focus, please," said Jerry sternly, turning off the projector. The handsome face disappeared. "Don't let his good looks fool you. That face belongs to one of the world's most dangerous criminals. He is known as Casanova Carl. Although he is very young—not much older than you, as a matter of fact—he is a master thief."

"What does he do? Rob banks?" asked Alex.

"Not exactly. He specializes in winning the hearts of rich young women. He asks them to marry him and then robs them of their fortunes. Then he vanishes without a trace."

"Lame-o!" said Clover disgustedly.

"Yes," agreed Jerry. "And Casanova Carl is no ordinary petty thief. WOOHP operatives have discovered that he has a personal issue with Valentine's Day in particular. His criminal activity seems to spike at this time of the year. It seems that Carl was a rather, uh, unattractive boy back when he was in junior high."

"Really? You'd never know!" said Sam.

"Well, it seems that one day he was publicly humiliated. He gave a valentine to a popular eighth-grade girl. She tore it up in front of everyone! He was laughed at."

"Harsh," said Clover.

"Indeed. He never quite recovered from the incident. As a result, he vowed to revenge himself by breaking the hearts—and stealing the fortunes—of as many women as he can!"

"In other words, the man has some serious interpersonal relationship issues to work out," said Sam.

Jerry nodded and flipped the projector back on. The handsome face appeared on the screen again. "This will be a fairly simple mission," he continued. "I need you to find a box of Valentine's chocolates and bring them back here to me."

"Oh, poor Jerry!" said Alex. "Didn't you get enough valentines this year?"

Jerry shook his head. "This is a special box. It contains some important information. Inside that box lies the secret password to the computer file that accesses the national treasury of the small nation of Malrovia."

"Okay, I must have dozed off during

geography the day we learned where that was," said Clover.

Jerry flicked to the next slide. A map of Europe appeared. "It's here," he said, pointing to a tiny country in the southeastern region. "Our WOOHP operatives have informed us that Casanova Carl managed to get Princess Sofia, the reigning head of state of Malrovia, to fall in love with him. Believing he would marry her, she revealed the means of obtaining the secret password. Should he learn this password, Carl could drain her country's treasury. The entire economy of Malrovia would collapse. And if he succeeds with this country, the consequences would be enormous for the rest of Europe and, yes, the world."

"Duh . . . why don't they just change the password?" Sam suggested.

"To do so the princess would have to tell her treasury secretary what happened. She is highly embarrassed about having been duped. She does not wish her staff to know that she has breached national security through a girlish crush. She has asked WOOHP to solve the situation quietly. In her opinion, if the news media were to find out what she has done, her country would be the laughingstock of Europe."

"Okay, so what do we do?" asked Sam.

"The password is hidden inside a heart-shaped box of Valentine's Day chocolates such as this one."

Jerry clicked to the next slide, which showed a shiny red box with a ribbon on it.

"The princess's personal secretary unknowingly gave the chocolates to Carl's accomplice, a young man known only as Harry the Hottie. At this very moment, Harry is on his way to Paris. He is scheduled to pass the chocolates along to Casanova Carl this afternoon. Carl is the only person—aside from the princess—who knows how to decode the password. Your job is to intercept the password before Carl gets ahold of it."

"Ooooh!" squealed Alex. "I love Paris! It's the City of Love!"

"Yes, well, there won't be time for that," grumbled Jerry. He glanced at his watch. "Your Spy Plane will be leaving very soon."

"So much for finding something to wear to the dance," said Clover, sighing.

"After you have secured the chocolates, bring them back to WOOHP headquarters," said Jerry. "We will return them to the princess. And before you go, I have a few gadgets for you to help you on the mission."

The girls sat up to listen to their instructions.

"This is a Laser Lipstick," said Jerry. He pulled off the top and gave the base a twist. An orange beam of light shot out, burning a hole in the projection screen. "Oops," he muttered to himself, turning off the laser beam. "And this," he said, holding up an sporty ladies' wristwatch, "is an object-retrieval device. Simply aim it at the object in question, open up the watch face, and . . ." He had pointed the watch at a portrait of WOOHP's founder that was hanging on the wall. A thin wire shot out of the watch,

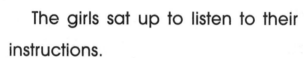

wrapped itself around the portrait, snapped the portrait off the wall, and zipped it into Jerry's waiting hands.

"Way cool," said Alex.

"And this is an Exploding Sleeping-Gas Barrette," he went on. "Very effective in putting your enemies to sleep in order to allow you to escape."

"I could use that in science lab," muttered Clover.

Jerry held up another gadget. "This is a surveillance heart-shaped locket. It has a very powerful microphone inside."

Then he unlocked a safe and pulled out a gold bracelet. "This bracelet contains a mini grappling hook with a strong steel cable to get you out of a tight fix. Oh, yes, and here are three pairs of Suction Cup Go-Go Boots."

Jerry quickly handed the rest of the items to the girls. "Now hurry, ladies. Your flight is leaving momentarily!"

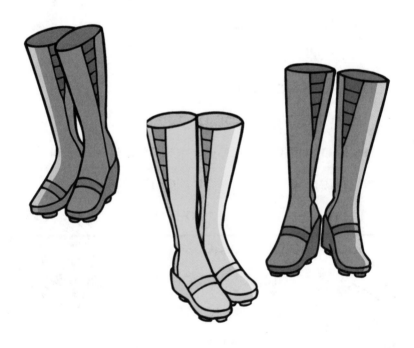

CHAPTER FOUR

A park in Paris, 4:53 p.m.

"Great," said Clover glumly. "Here we are in the City of Love. But are we sitting in quaint cafes checking out cute French guys? No. We're climbing trees." She, Sam, and Alex were crouching in a large tree just above a park bench. They were waiting for Carl and Harry's chocolate handoff.

"Ouch! This tree branch is giving me a

mega wedgie," complained Alex.

"It won't be much longer," said Sam. "It's nearly time for the handoff. Do you have the SpyJet fueled up, Clover?"

"Affirmative," replied Clover.

"Pssst!" said Sam. "Someone's coming!"

The girls peered through the leaves to see a man approaching the park bench. Even from a distance they saw that he was tall and broad-shouldered. As he approached, they recognized the young man from the pictures Jerry had shown them.

"It's Casanova Carl!" whispered Alex.

"It's kind of a shame that he's a sinister mastermind with serious dating issues who's hatched an evil scheme to destabilize the world economy," said Clover with a sigh. "He's soooo hot."

"Snap out of it and keep an eye out for Harry the Hottie!" Sam hissed at her.

Carl walked casually over to the bench just below where the girls were staked out. He sat down and opened a newspaper.

A moment later another man appeared on the path, coming from the other direction. He was also young, not quite as tall as Carl, but nearly as handsome. His blond hair ruffled in the light breeze. Under his arm was a large red heart-shaped box.

Alex gestured toward the second man urgently with her chin. The other girls nodded. He had to be Harry the Hottie. They watched the second man amble casually toward the park bench. He stopped under their tree, pulled out a cell phone, and pretended to dial.

Casanova Carl folded up his newspaper, stood up, and took a step toward Harry.

"NOW!" yelled Sam to the other two. Quick as a flash, Sam was running straight down the trunk of the tree in her specially outfitted go-go boots.

The men whirled in her direction, taken by surprise. Alex used that moment to open her watch and aim it at the box of chocolates. In an instant, the silver wire had curled around the box under Harry's arm and was zinging its way back into Alex's waiting arms. She tossed the box to Clover, who did a backflip out of the tree and landed in the driver's seat

of the SpyJet, which had been idling quietly behind a bush. Clover revved up the engine.

"Come on!" yelled Clover. Alex and Sam leaped into the passenger seats. Clover handed the box of chocolates to Alex.

The two men yelled with rage and started after the girls, but Clover fired up the SpyJet and zoomed off.

"Jerry was right. That was easy," Alex said, giggling as they sped along next to the river. "We'll be back home with plenty of time for relaxed shopping and beautifying before the dance tomorrow night."

"Plenty of time? As if," said Clover. "I am totally overdue for a deep-cleansing treatment."

"Um, not so fast," said Sam, turning around and looking behind her. "We have company."

Sure enough, Carl and Harry were chasing

them in their own version of the SpyJet.

"Lose 'em, Clover!" said Alex.

Clover pushed the lever up a couple of notches and they zoomed forward with a burst of speed. The SpyJet careened around a corner and swooped under an arched bridge spanning the river. Then it zoomed toward the Eiffel Tower, which suddenly loomed in front of them. Just when it seemed they were going to crash right into it, Clover pulled back on another lever. The SpyJet pointed its nose vertically in the air. They shot up and over the monument. Then, in a graceful swoop, they descended downward toward another part

of the river. The SpyJet came to rest between two flowering trees, causing a family of ducks to squawk indignantly and waddle away.

"Great job, Clover! You lost them!" said Sam. "Now let's have a look inside that box of chocolates."

CHAPTER FIVE

Eagerly Alex untied the ribbon and pulled off the top of the box. The three girls stared down into the contents.

"All I see are chocolates," said Sam.

"Me too," said Clover. She pushed them around a bit in the box. There was nothing but a collection of round, square, and rectangular chocolates sitting inside crimped brown wrappers.

"They don't even look like good chocolates," Alex said, sniffing.

Clover took one out of the box. She peered at it closely. Then she popped it into her mouth. A look of disgust crossed her face, and she swallowed with difficulty. "Eeew! I hate the ones with fruity cherry goo on the inside."

"Me too," agreed Alex.

"I guess we should radio Jerry and tell him the mission was a failure," said Sam. "His WOOHP operatives must have been wrong. There is definitely no password in this box of chocolates." She flipped open her powder compact, and a microphone rose up. "No password here, Jerry," she said.

"Don't be too sure," Jerry's voice crackled out of the tiny microphone. "Remember, it's carefully hidden somewhere."

"I don't think so," said

Sam dubiously. "It looks like plain old ordinary chocolate to me."

"And not very good chocolate!" added Clover, leaning indignantly toward the microphone. "Why, we . . ."

"Incoming!" yelled Alex. But it was too late. Pink smoke was suddenly rising up all around. It was spewing out of a wind-up duck, which someone had tossed toward them. The girls fell to the ground.

"Oh, I can't move. . . ." said Sam. It was paralysis gas! The other two lay next to her, also unable to move their arms and legs.

The compact had fallen from Sam's hand and was beeping over and over. But none of the girls could move a muscle.

Just then a long shadow fell over them. Casanova Carl stepped out from behind one of the trees. "So. You thought you could outwit me, you silly bunch of girls!" he said. "As if you three could be a match for my talents!"

"What talents would those be?" said Clover sarcastically. "Winding up toy ducks?"

Carl scowled at her and a twitch appeared in his left eye. "You look like the sort of girls who were mean to unpopular boys back in junior high school." He pulled himself together and called loudly, "Harry! The chocolates!"

Harry appeared and plucked the box of chocolates from Alex's motionless hands.

"I don't think you're going to find what you're looking for," said Alex.

Carl ignored her. "Start eating!" he commanded Harry.

Obediently Harry began taking bites of chocolates, then throwing the half-eaten pieces back in the box.

"Eeeeew!" said all three girls disgustedly.

Harry appeared to agree, as his face began turning a faint shade of green. "Feel sick," he mumbled. "Here . . . you gotta help me!" he growled at Carl, shoving the box toward his partner.

"Don't worry, girls," said Carl, taking the box from Harry. "Feeling should return to your arms and legs in an hour or so." He popped a chocolate into his mouth, then another, and another. "By that time, we'll be long gone!" He laughed as evilly as he could with a mouthful of chocolate. Then he and Harry hurried away.

It took at least an hour before the girls had

enough feeling return in their bodies to be able to sit up.

"Ow! My legs are so stiff!" said Clover. "I can't believe I ever thought he was hot! Although," she added thoughtfully, "he does have fabulous eyes."

"Why on earth would they stuff themselves full of those icky chocolates?" Alex wanted to know. "It's definitely not going to help their complexions!"

Sam's pressed-powder compact began beeping again. "That's Jerry," she said, picking it up from the ground where she had dropped it. "He's probably wondering what happened to us." She flipped it open and Jerry's voice immediately poured out.

"Girls, I heard what happened!" he said. "They've taken the chocolates, haven't they?"

"Well, yeah, but there's no password, duh," said Clover. "And then they started eating them. Even worse, they put the half-eaten pieces back in the box. It was, like, totally gross."

"Do listen!" said Jerry's voice urgently. "Did any of you girls eat the chocolates?"

Alex and Sam looked at Clover.

"Uh, maybe just one," Clover said. "Why do you ask?"

"Because the princess just informed us that the password is encrypted inside a chocolate-covered cherry!" replied Jerry. "There's only one in the box. It uses time-delay technology. Brilliant, really. After it is eaten, the chocolate enters the bloodstream of the person who ate it and reassembles the epidermal cells in the lower thoracic region to form the encrypted message!"

"Uh, let's try speaking English, Jer," Clover prompted.

"It's an edible password! The code will gradually start to appear on the midriff of the eater. After about twenty-four hours it will be fully visible!" Jerry said.

"Okay, so now I'm officially freaked out," said Clover, looking down at her stomach.

"And so if the chocolate that you ate turns out to be the one carrying the password," Jerry was continuing, "then as soon as Carl discovers it's not in the box, he'll realize one of you girls must have eaten the chocolate. He and Harry will come after . . ."

"AAAAAAHHHH!!!" shrieked all three girls at the same time. A large net had been dropped on them from a silent hovercraft that had flown over their heads. They were caught!

CHAPTER SIX

A castle dungeon, Malrovia, 8:00 p.m.

"I guess you girls are not quite as dumb as I thought," said Carl grudgingly. He was standing in front of the girls in a small, damp room. They were tied together with a rope.

"Since I don't know which one of you ate the password, I'll just have to keep all three of you around until it shows up. But when it does . . ." He drew a finger across his throat and chuckled.

The girls rolled their eyes.

"And now if you'll excuse me, it is time for dinner," he continued. "I have a date right here in this castle. The Baroness Felicia de LaRoche-DuBoef believes I own the place! Little does she know that I've temporarily 'borrowed' it from another fiancée of mine. The baroness seems eager to share her fortune with the man of her dreams. And that would be, let's see . . . oh, yes! Me!" He laughed maniacally, straightened his bowtie, and then walked out of the room.

"Cute but creepy . . . in a major way," said Clover.

"Yup," agreed Alex. "And he has real issues with dating."

Sam had been fiddling around with her laser lipstick. She finally managed to get the right angle and cut through the rope that bound her wrists. The rope fell to the floor. Quickly Sam untied the other two.

Alex tiptoed over to the small barred window in the doorway and peered out. "There are at least four goons guarding our cell," she reported.

"Anything yet, Clover?" asked Sam.

Clover pulled up her shirt. "It looks like some letters are starting to appear faintly," she said, "but I can't see what they say. Especially upside down." She frowned. "It's bad enough that we're going to deliver the password into this bad guy's hands, destabilize the world economy, and then die. But you know what's the worst of it? We are totally going to miss the Valentine's Day dance."

"Not necessarily," said Sam. "Carl and Harry

won't be back to check on us anytime soon. We have at least a few hours before your password shows up. And remember, we still have our gadgets. Those two were too busy with the chocolates to bother checking us for weapons."

Sam pulled out her laser lipstick. She put a finger to her lips, and tiptoed over to the barred window cut into the cell door. A bright orange light appeared at the tip of her lipstick, and she quietly began lasering through the bars.

Clover hurried over and flipped open her object-retrieval watch. Even in the dim light of the corridor, she could see that the guards were busy playing cards. She spied the keys to their cell on the wall nearby, and pressed the button on her watch. In a flash, the keys were in her hands.

"Catch, Alex!" said Clover. She tossed the keys to Alex as she pulled a barrette from her hair.

"Hey!" yelled the guards, scrambling to their feet as Alex reached through the now-open window to unlock the door.

But the guards didn't get far. Clover tossed the barrette onto the floor in front of them, and it exploded into a dense cloud of sleeping gas. In a moment the guards lay snoring on the floor and the girls were freed.

"That should keep them quiet for about eight hours," said Sam.

The girls were breathing through their upturned collars, which were made of a special air-filtering material.

"Where are we, I wonder?" said Alex, looking up and down the corridor. "This castle is so last century!"

Sam was looking up thoughtfully at a vent in the wall above them. "I wonder where that air-conditioning duct leads."

"Air conditioning in an old castle?" scoffed Clover. "As if!"

"It looks as though it's been renovated recently," said Sam. "I'm going to do some listening-in."

Sam activated her go-go boots and suction-cup-walked up the wall. Then she unclasped her heart-shaped locket and slipped it through the vent openings.

"I hear him!" she hissed to the others, listening through the earpiece. "He's having dinner with the baroness just upstairs from here! We've got to stop him before he tricks her out of her fortune!"

"Let's roll," said Clover. She and Alex scaled the wall in seconds. Soon the three of them were crawling through the tunnel in the direction of the voices.

CHAPTER SEVEN

"Darling," came a breathy voice from inside the room. The girls were crouched in the air duct, listening. "I cannot live apart from you for a moment longer. When shall we be married?"

"Soon, my dear, very soon," came the reply. The girls recognized Carl's voice, although it was quite different from the one he had been using with them not long before. Now it was velvety and smooth. "You have only to authorize the transaction with your Swiss bank, darling. I will take care of all the wedding details. My butler here has the papers for you to sign."

"Look!" whispered Alex, peeking through the vent. "Harry the Hottie is posing as the butler!"

"Of course, of course," replied the baroness. "How much did you say you needed for our wedding expenses? Ten million, was it?"

"That should do for now," replied Carl smoothly.

The girls heard a loud clank as Harry dropped a plate onto his tray.

"Real suave, Harry," whispered Clover sarcastically.

"Very well, darling," said the baroness. The girls heard her moving to the table to sign the papers.

Sam nodded to the other two. In a flash

they crashed through the vent and sprang into the room. "Not so fast, Madame!" called Sam loudly. "These men are *not* who you think they are!"

Before the astonished baroness could say a word, Harry bolted for the door. Sam tripped Harry so that he sprawled on the floor.

Carl lunged for the girls with a snarl of rage. But they sidestepped him quickly. The baron-

ess found her voice. "D-darling!" she said, fal-tering. Then she gasped. Carl had pulled out a weapon! The girls froze.

"I'm sorry it had to come to this, my dear," he said to the baroness. "But unfortunately these pesky girls have spoiled our wedding plans. You will just have to sign the papers anyway. Then my butler and I will be leaving."

Clover snorted. "And you think you're going

to get away with this because . . ."

"Because it is now necessary to lock my beloved baroness in the dungeon . . . indefinitely! No one will come looking for her, believing she has eloped with the handsomest man in the world!" said Carl with an ugly laugh.

The baroness gasped.

"And as for you!" he said to the girls. "I'll take care of you once and for all! Care for a little dip? Bwah-hah-hah-hah!"

Carl touched a button under the desk. The floor slid open below the girls' feet. With surprised shrieks, they tumbled down a steep incline, straight toward the castle's moat.

As she slid downward, Sam could see the open mouths of several alligators. They thrashed their tails, eagerly awaiting the girls' arrival. Just then Sam remembered the bracelet Jerry had given her. She quickly shot a perfectly aimed grappling hook at a gargoyle, then grabbed Alex by the wrist. Alex, in turn, grabbed Clover by the ankle—and just in the nick of time! Clover hung inches above the snapping jaws of the alligators. After a while the alligators slowly slithered below the surface of the moat.

"I thought we were going to be 'gator food for sure!" said Alex with a sigh of relief.

"Yeah," agreed Clover. "Nice work, Sammy."

"Come on," said Sam, activating her suction-cup go-go boots again and starting to climb up the castle wall. "We've got some bad guys to catch."

CHAPTER EIGHT

WOOHP Headquarters, 6:00 p.m.,
Valentine's Day

"Excellent work, ladies," said Jerry to the girls, who sat sprawled on the couches in his office. "Carl and Harry are behind bars, and the fortunes of the baroness and the princess are safe."

"I'm, like, totally happy for them," said Alex glumly. "At least someone is having a nice Valentine's Day."

Clover and Sam sighed in agreement.

"Why, whatever is the matter?" asked Jerry.

"We have absolutely nothing to wear to the dance, which starts in an hour!" said Clover.

"I wouldn't be too concerned," Jerry said with a chuckle.

"Hello? We are in the middle of a fashion meltdown and you're laughing?" said Clover accusingly.

Jerry stood up and walked over to a closet. "I forgot to tell you. The princess was so grateful for what you did for her that she sent along some thank-you presents. I trust these are the right size and all?" He slid open one of the doors of the closet. Hanging inside were several dozen dresses, all fabulously cut and in the latest styles.

The girls' jaws dropped.

"Oh, and the Baroness sent you a little something as well," said Jerry with a twinkle in his eye. He slid open the door on the other side of the closet. Stacked floor to ceiling were boxes and boxes of shoes in each of the girls' sizes.

"Jerry," said Sam when she had found her voice. " This is huge. This is like . . . epic."

"I need a minute to process this!" said Alex, looking as though she was in a state of shock.

"I'd cry with happiness, but my mascara's not waterproof," said Clover.

The girls rushed to try on the dresses and then started trying on shoes.

Suddenly Alex gasped. "Hey, Clover," she said. "What's that?" She pointed to Clover's belly.

Clover peered down. The words BE MY
VALENTINE had appeared on her midriff in
sparkly letters.

"That was the password?" said Alex, laughing. "Who knew?"

"Oh, no!" cried Clover. "Now I have to find an outfit that will cover up the words!"

"No, Clover, that password *is* the ultimate fashion accessory," said Sam. "And you can show it off tonight wearing this dress!" she added. "Happy Valentine's Day, you trendsetter!"